D1338307

For David

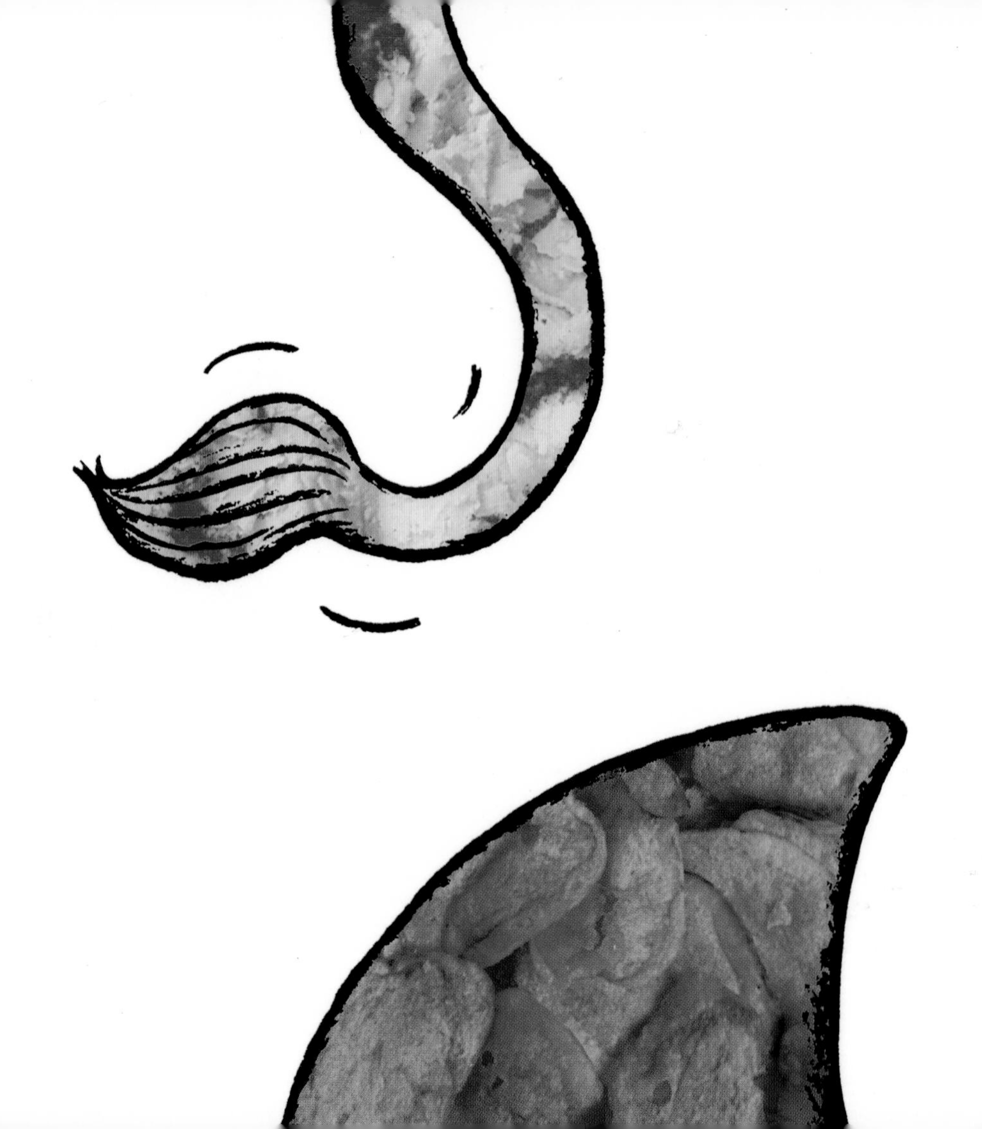

I went to the Zoopermarket

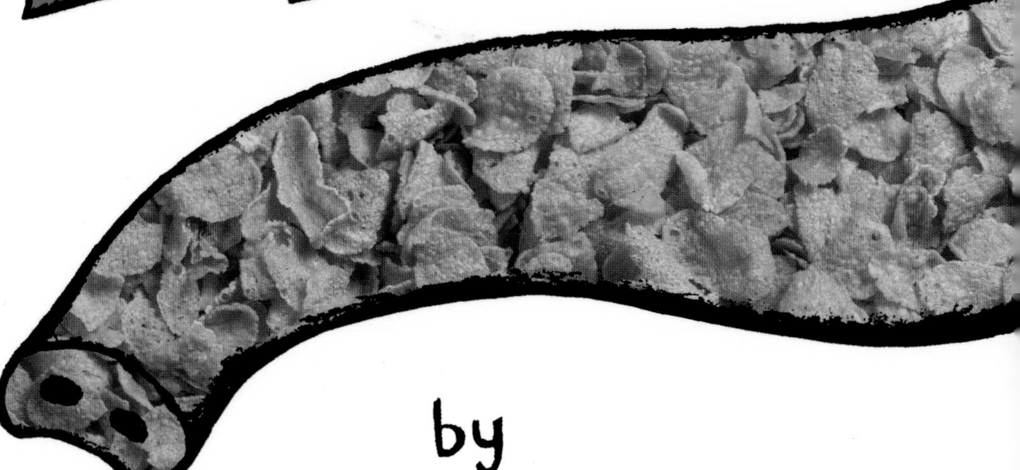

by

Nick Sharratt

SCHOLASTIC
PRESS

I went to
the Zoopermarket
and I bought
some BARMY BISCUITS.

quack!
quack!
QUACKERS

I went to
the Zoopermarket
and I bought
some CRAZY CRISPS.

fangtastic
flavour!

I went to
the Zoopermarket
and I bought
a DAFT DESSERT.

ooh! ooh! ooh!
APE-RICOT YOGHURT

I went to
the Zoopermarket
and I bought
the ODDEST ONIONS.

Ouch!

I went to
the Zoopermarket
and I bought
some EXCITING
ICE-CREAM.

raaargh!

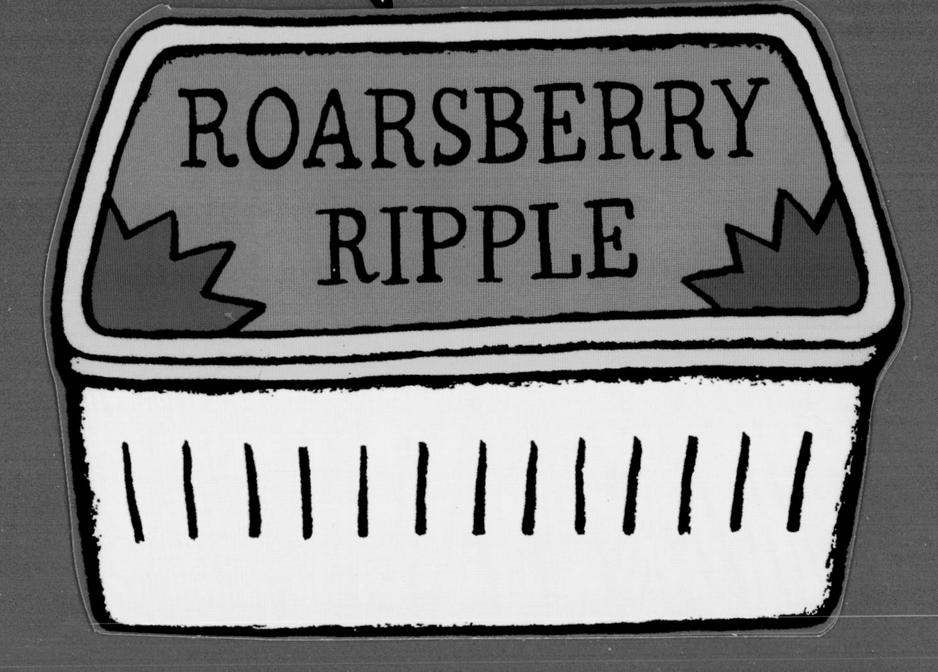
ROARSBERRY
RIPPLE

I went to
the Zoopermarket
and I bought
some FABBO FRUIT.

KANGA-
ROO BARB

boing!
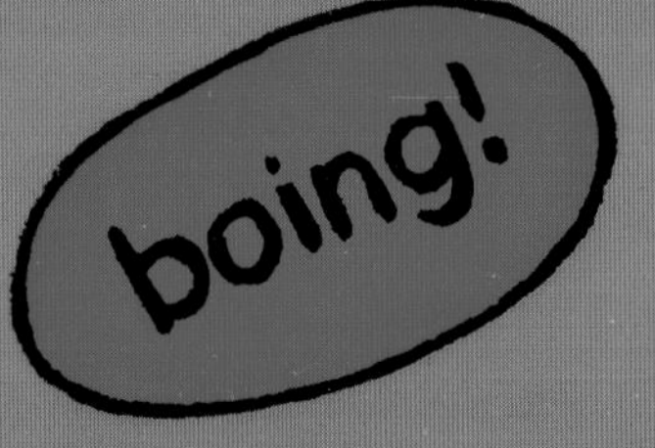
boing!

boing!

I went to
the Zoopermarket
and I bought
some SNAZZY SWEETS.

snappetizing!

CROCOLATE
DROPS

I went to
the Zoopermarket
and I bought
some FUNNY FIZZ.

croak!
croak!
CROAKER-
COLA

I went to
the Zoopermarket
and I bought
a box of cornflakes –
JUMBO SIZE!

Scholastic Children's Books,
Commonwealth House, 1-19 New Oxford Street,
London WC1A 1NU, UK
a division of Scholastic Ltd

London ~ New York ~ Toronto ~ Sydney ~ Auckland
Mexico City ~ New Delhi ~ Hong Kong

First published in the UK by Scholastic Publications, 1995
This miniature edition published by Scholastic Ltd, 2000

Computer manipulation by Peter Cannings

ISBN 0 439 01361 5

Printed in China

2 4 6 8 10 9 7 5 3 1